First Letters

Trace over the handwriting patterns
and letters with your special pen.
Try to start at the big dot each time!

Note to parents: when red arrows are shown, left-handed
writers should follow these to form their letters.

a

is for
ant

a a a a

Finish the word.

apple

 Practise with Peppa

.........pple

b

is for
balloon

b b b b

Finish the word.

ball

 Practise with Peppa

.........all

c

is for
car

c c c c

Finish the word.

cake

.......ake

d

is for
dinosaur

d d d d

Finish the word.

duck

Practise with Peppa

.......uck

e

is for
envelope

e   e   e   e

Finish the word.

 gg

Practise with Peppa

.........gg

f

is for
fire engine

f   f   f   f

Finish the word.

ish

Practise with Peppa

.........ish

g

is for
guitar

g g g g

Finish the word.

 Practise with Peppa

 **grass** ....rass

h

is for
house

h h h h

Finish the word.

 Practise with Peppa

 **hat** ....at

i

is for

insects

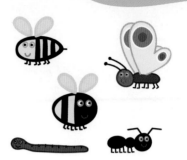

i   i   i   i

Finish the word.

 ice cream   ......ce cream

j

is for

jumbo jet

j   j   j   j

Finish the word.

Practise with Peppa

 jelly   ....elly

k

is for
keys

k   k   k   k   k

Finish the word.

kite

 Practise with Peppa

.....ite

l

is for
ladybird

l   l   l   l   l

 Practise with Peppa

Finish the word.

lunchbox   .....unchbox

m

is for
mirror

m   m m m m

Finish the word.

m.**ud**   ....**ud**

n

is for
newspaper

n   n n n

Finish the word.

n.**est**   ....**est**

O is for octopus

o   o o o

Finish the word.

orange   ....range

p is for pencil

p   p p p

Finish the word.

Practise with Peppa

 parrot   ......arrot

q

is for
queen

q   q   q   q

Finish the word.

 Practise with Peppa

  quilt

.......uilt

r

is for
rocket

r   r   r   r

Finish the word.

 Practise with Peppa

 rainbow

.....ainbow

S

is for
sandwich

s

s s s

Finish the word.

 Practise with Peppa

 star

..........**tar**

t

is for
train

t

t t t

Finish the word.

 Practise with Peppa

 teddy

..........**eddy**

u

is for
umbrella

u   u   u   u

Finish the word.

 **underwear**

Practise with Peppa

.......nderwear

V

is for
van

v   v   v   v

Finish the word.

Practise with Peppa

vase

.........ase

W is for watering can

W w w w

Finish the word.

wellies

.........ellies

X is for xylophone

X x x x

Finish the word.

box

Practise with Peppa

.........ox

y

is for
yellow

y y y y

Finish the word.

yacht

 Practise with Peppa

.......acht

z

is for
zebra

z z z z

Finish the word.

zig-zag

 Practise with Peppa

.......ig-zag

Here are some words from the book.
Can you draw the right letter shape at the start of each one?

 .... adybird

.... ocket

 .... nderwear

 .... alloon

 .... ctopus

 .... elly

Trace the letter shapes of the whole alphabet.
It's fun to practise with Peppa!

Snort!

Snort!